DON'T BLINK NOW, 'CAUSE WE ARE LIVE FROM PARIS! YO PEEPS!
Ladyblog
Pharaoh
Created by: Thomas Astruc
Comics adaptation by: Nicole D'Andria
Written by: Cédric Bacconnier
Art arranged by: Cheryl Black
Lettered by: Justin Birch

Ladyblog
ALYA HERE, BRINGING YOU THE ONE AND ONLY LADYBLOG!

Ladyblog
GASP
WHAT IS THAT?! LADYBUG IN ACTION!

Ladyblog
HANG ON, UZ WE'RE OIN' FOR A RIIIDE!

Histoire
Ladyblog
FREAK.
OUT.

Ladyblog
WHAT YOU GOT HERE S NO ORDINARY OOK... IT'S A 10TH GRADE HISTORY BOOK!
Histoire

AND I SHOULD KNOW, CUZ I'VE GOT THIS VERY SAME BOOK!

Ladyblog
Pharaons
Accueil
Photos
Videos
Archives
Ladybug collégienne ?
COULD OUR VERY OWN LADYBUG BE A HIGH-SCHOOL STUDENT... IN REAL LIFE?!

I TOLD YOU, FROM DAY ONE, TIKKI...
...I'M A TOTAL KLUTZ!

WHAT'S DONE IS DONE. WE CAN'T CHANGE WHAT HAPPENED.
WE CAN ONLY MOVE FORWARD.

ALYA MUST NOT FIND OUT WHO YOU ARE.
YOU KNOW HOW PERSISTENT SHE CAN BE WITH HER BLOG TOTALLY DEDICATED TO LADYBUG!

BUT HOW? MAYBE I'M N CUT OUT FOR WHOLE LADY THING...

OU ARE CHOSEN ONE ARINETTE!
IT WILL ALL WORK OUT. TRUST ME! EVERYONE HAS A PAST THEY CAN LEARN FROM.

Accueil Photos Videos Archives
Ladybug collégienne ?
ICK
CLICK
CLICK
PHARAONS
THIS'LL SHOW YOU WHY.

AN EXHIBITION ON THE LOUVRE? ON THE PHARAOH TUTUKAMUN?

WHAT DOES THAT HAVE TO DO WITH MY BOOK AND ALYA?
YOU MUST PERSUADE ALYA TO GO THERE WITH YOU, AND MAKE SURE SHE BRINGS THE BOOK!
YOU'LL TELL HER YOU FOUND OUT SOMETHING ABOUT LADYBUG.

AT THE MUSEUM?
YOU'LL SEE.
HOW?!
PHARA

I DON'T KNOW HOW I'M GONNA CONVINCE ALYA TO GO TO AN EGYPTIAN EXHIBIT...
PHARAONS
...MUCH LESS CONVINCE HER THAT I'M NOT LADYBUG!
SHE WILL BE INTERESTED.
AND SO WILL YOU. PROMISE!

33 Gare d'Austerlitz
CAN YOU BELIEVE IT?! ALL I GOTTA DO IS FIND OUT WHO THIS HISTORY BOOK BELONGS TO AND BAM!
I FIGURE OUT LADYBUG'S TRUE IDENTITY!
UH... YOU REALLY THINK YOU CAN FIGURE OUT WHO LADYBUG IS FROM A TEXTBOOK THAT EVERY HIGH SCHOOL STUDENT OWNS?
YEP!
'CUZ OUR SCHOOL IS THE ONLY SCHOOL THAT USES THAT BOOK!
HA!
SO, ALL I GOTTA DO IS FIND OUT WHICH GIRL IN 10TH GRADE LOST HER BOOK LAST WEEK.
THERE ARE 43 GIRLS, NOT COUNTING MYSELF-

42! NOT COUNTING YOU OR ME!
YESTERDAY, SOMEBODY DIDN'T HAVE HER TEXTBOOK IN CLASS...
EEEE!
W- I- I LEFT IT AT HOME! YOU KNOW I ALWAYS FORGET MY STUFF!
HMM...
HA HA HA! JUST MESSING WITH YOU, MARINETTE!

EXCUSE ME.
THERE! AS YOU KNOW, THE ONE WITH THE SCEPTER IS TUTANKHAMUN, THE FIRST.
AND THERE, PPOSITE, IS NEFERTITI, PRINCESS. THERE ARE ACTLY 100 MUMMIES BESIDE THEM.
SHE DIED SEVERAL YEARS BEFORE HIM, AND THE SUN GOD, RA, TOOK HER AS HIS GODDESS.
YES, I KNOW ALL THAT!
I'M THE DIRECTOR OF THIS EXHIBITION, REMEMBER?

THEN YOU ALSO KNOW THAT TUTANKHAMUN WANTED TO BRING HIS PRINCESS BACK TO LIFE BY OFFERING THE SUN GOD A NEW WIFE.
THIS SCENE ILLUSTRATES THE RITUAL HE DEVISED.
NOBODY HAS EVER FULLY DECIPHERED THE HIEROGLYPHICS. BUT I HAVE!
IT'S A MAGIC CHANT THAT NEEDS TO BE RECITED IN ORDER TO COMPLETE THE RITUAL. I'M SURE OF IT!
HE KINDA REMINDS ME OF SOMEONE ELSE WITH CRAZY IDEAS... YOU!
PFFF... YOU MIGHT "THINK" MY THEORIES ABOUT LADYBUG ARE CRAZY, BUT YOU WATCH, GIRL! I'LL PROVE YOU WRONG!

JALIL, THESE TYPES OF FRESCOES ARE ALMOST ALWAYS THE ILLUSTRATION OF A *LEGEND.*
THEY CALL IT A LEGEND FOR A REASON.
THAT'S WHAT EVERYONE THINKS - BUT I KNOW IT'S REAL! I CAN PROVE IT!
REALLY? AND EXACTLY HOW ARE YOU GOING TO PROVE IT?
I JUST NEED TO GET MY HANDS ON TUTANKHAMUN'S SCEPTER AND RECITE THE SPELL-
ARE YOU SERIOUS?!
DON'T EVEN THINK OF TOUCHING THAT SCEPTER!
I'D LOSE MY JOB ON THE SPOT!
IT'S A PRICELESS, HISTORICAL OBJECT... *NOT* A TOY!
C'MON AD, WE E TO TRY UT THE SPELL!
WHAT IF ANKHAMUN FOUND OUT TO BRING OPLE BACK O LIFE?!
LISTEN, JALIL!
THAT'S ENOUGH!
GET YOUR HEAD OUT OF THOSE PAPYRUS SCROLLS, AND FOCUS ON THE REAL WORLD... *THIS ONE!*

THERE'S NOTHING WRONG WITH LIVING OUT A FANTASY...
...ESPECIALLY WHEN I CAN MAKE IT A *REALITY.*

WWZZING
FLY AWAY MY EVIL AKUMA, AND TRANSFORM THAT YOUNG MAN!

FWWSH
PHARAOH, I AM HAWK MOTH. I HAVE ENDOWED YOU WITH THE MAGICAL POWER OF THE ANCIENT GODS.
YOU MUST DO ME A FAVOR IN RETURN FOR THIS GIFT.
MY PRECIOUS NEFERTITI WILL COME BACK TO LIFE!

TUT...
...GIVE ME TIME!

ZWWING

SWOOSH

BLOOP

AAAH!
RAONS
SWOOSH

RAONS
BLOOP
HEY!

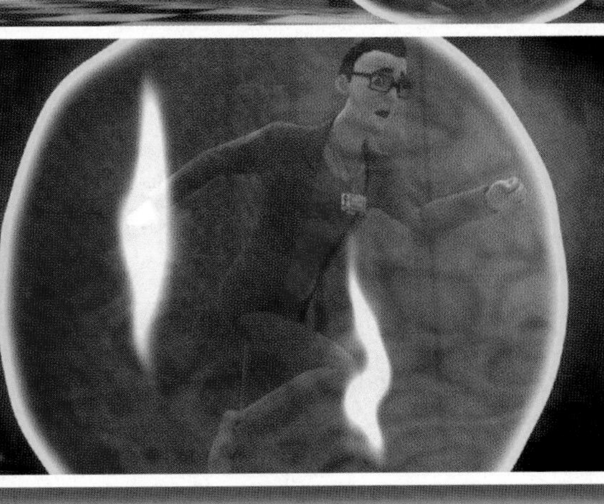

INCOMING!
NOW THIS IS BLOG WORTHY!
CLICK!
ALYA! HIDE!
HE'S USING THE BUBBLES TO SLOW DOWN TIME!
AND I THOUGHT TODAY WAS A TOTAL BUST!

GET OUT OF HERE!

FASTER!!!
SWOOSH
ZOOM

WE GOTTA TRANSFORM!

TIKKI...

...SPOTS ON!
TIN
FWWSH
SWISH

OMG! COMING TO YOU LIVE, LADYBLOG VIEWERS!
I'M AT THE SCENE, EVEN BEFORE LADYBUG OR CAT NOIR! THIS IS INSANE!
REC
WWZZING
HA HA HA HA!
WOW! I LOVE THE FACE CHANGES. YOU COULD USE THAT ONE!
...TIME TO TRANSFORM.

PLAG
CLAWS
FWWSH
TING

SWOOSH
WEEEE-OOOOOO
WEE-OOOO
OOF!

YOU KNOW THAT'S CONSIDERED STEALING!
ACTUALLY, I'M TAKING BACK WHAT RIGHTFULLY BELONGS TO ME.

...WHICH YOU'RE NOT!
BE IF YOU
E THE REAL
ARAOH...
WEE-OOOO

LOOK AT LADYBUG GO! IF I'M DREAMING, DON'T WAKE ME UP!
EEE!
LADYBUG WAVED AT ME.
NO WAY!
HYAAAH!
FWOOSH

SNAG!
HMPH!
AAAH!
WOAAAHH!
SLAM

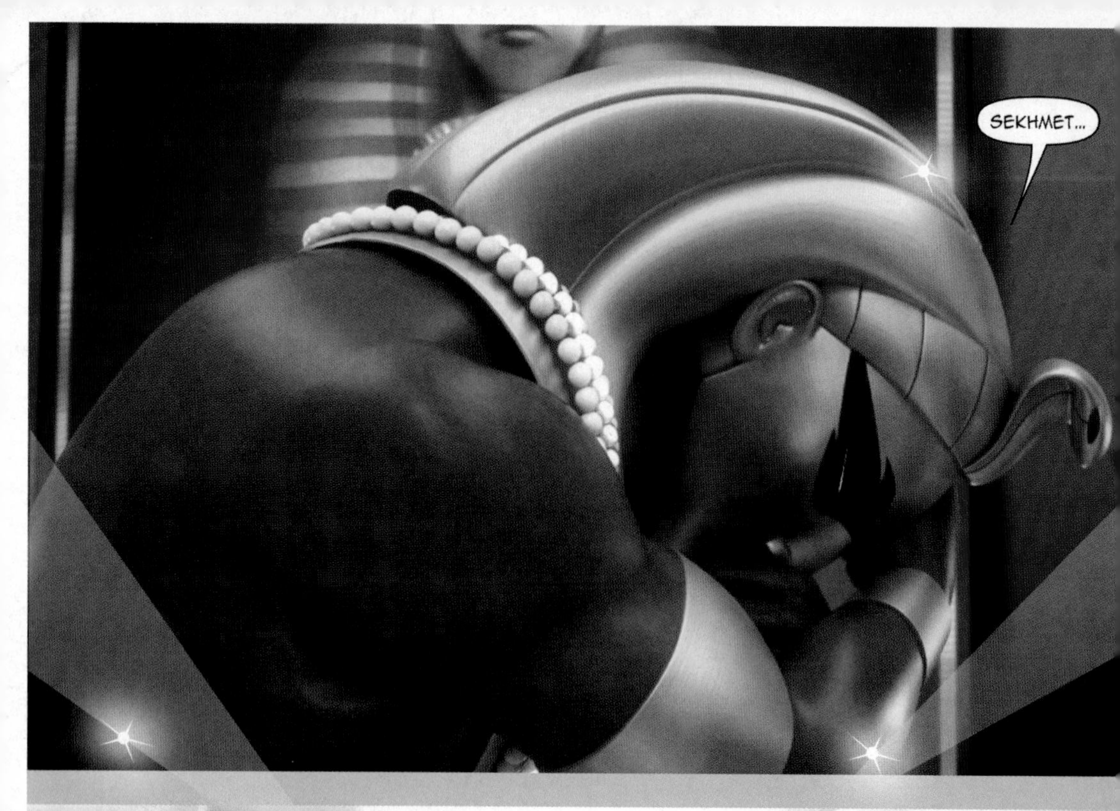
SEKHMET...

...GIVE ME YOUR STRENGTH!

SCREEEC

HOW NICE OF YOU TO HOLD THE DOOR OPEN FOR ME!
OOF!
ENJOY YOUR COFFIN!
WAAAH!
SLAM
THIS IS HECKA CRAZY!

KEEP YOUR EYES PEELED!

GASP
HIYA...
URK!

YOUR FACE... FATE HAS PLACED YOU ON MY PATH. COME WITH ME!

HEY! HANDS OFF THE THREADS!

I. CAN. WALK. MYSELF!

SERIOUSLY?!

HURR... URGH...

AH!

COUGH
COUGH

HIDING BEHIND AN INNOCENT BYSTANDER?! YOU'RE WEAK, PHARAOH!

I'M WAY MORE POWERFUL THAN YOU ARE!

SCREEECH

AND DON'T FORGET: ALL THE LATEST "BEHIND THE SCENES" ARE ON MY BLOOOOG!
THAT ALYA IS ONE BRAVE CHICK!
IF BY "BRAVE" MEAN "FEISTY,"

YUP, THAT'S HER!

COME ON, GET US OUTTA HERE, CAT NOIR!

YOUR WISH IS MY COMMAND!
CRUNCH!
CATACLYSM!

WOOOSH

SNAAAP!
HOW ARE WE GOING TO FIND THEM?!

ALYA'S GOT A LIVESTREAM ON HER BLOG!

HI EVERYONE!

Au secours !
ALYA HERE, LIVEBLOGGING FROM THE SHOULDER OF A TERRIFYING VILLAIN!

HUGE SCOOP TO COME, STAY TUNED!
BEEP
BEEP
BEEP
UH... GO AHEAD!
I'LL JOIN YOU AS SOON AS MY MIRACULOUS IS CHARGED UP AGAIN!

HURRY UP!
IT'S GOING TO TAKE BOTH OF US TO DEFEAT HIM!

HEY!
ON TO THE NEXT PHASE.
ANUBIS...
...BRING ME MUMMIES!
WWZZING

SKREEEEEE
SKREEEE
SKREEEEE

GASP
SOON, WE WILL BE TOGETHER AGAIN, MY NEFERTITI!
I WILL HOLD YOU ONCE MORE, MY LONG-LOST LOVE!
THIS GONNA ONE MA SCOO
UH... 'SCUSE ME, PHARAOH, BUT, UH...
...WHAT EXACTLY IS GOING ON?
I AM GOING TO CARRY OUT THE SACRED SPELL, TO BRING NEFERTITI BACK!
AH, HMMM... GOTCHA! YOU'RE TALKING ABOUT THE SPELL ON THE PAPYRUS RIGHT?

CORRECT! THE 100 MUMMIES AND THE OFFERING.
OFFERING? WHAT OFFERING?
MY OFFERING TO RA!
TO PERSUADE THE SUN GOD RA TO GIVE ME BACK MY SWEET PRINCESS, I MUST GIVE HIM SOMETHING IN RETURN.
A PURE SOUL!

DUDE, THAT'S HARD TO COME BY...
BUT I'VE ALREADY FOUND HER!
YOU LOOK SO MUCH LIKE HER!
SAY WHAAAAT?!?!
Au secours !
MWAHAHAHAHAH.
HOLD ON, ALYA!

WOOOAAHHHH...
BLOOP
OH NO!
I RAN *RIGHT* INTO ONE OF THOSE TIME BUBBLES. I'VE GOT TO GET OUT OF THIS!
BAM!
LADYBUG, THIS IS ALYA!
u secours !
I JUST FOUND OUT *I'M* THE SACRIFICIAL OFFERING FOR THE SUN GOD! PLEASE... HURRY!
I'M NEARLY THERE!

LOOKS LIKE I'M JUST IN TIME!

SPLOOSH!

WHOA!

THANKS FOR WAITING AROUND FOR ME!

NO PROBLEM!

WE'VE GOT TO FIND THE HIDDEN AKUMA AND FREE IT BEFORE HE SACRIFICES THAT POOR GIRL!
I DON'T SEE HER OR PHARAOH.
WE CAN SEE MORE FROM THE ROOF!
OVER THERE!

HMPH?
WHOA, BACK UP! WHO'S THAT GODDESS CHICK WITH THE BLACK SPOTS?!
THERE, ON YOUR PAPYRUS!
LADYBUG, MY SWORN ENEMY! MY NEMESIS MAY HAVE KEPT ME FROM CARRYING OUT MY RITUAL 5000 YEARS AGO...
CRUSH!
...BUT SHE WILL NOT STOP NEFERTITI FROM COMING BACK TO ME THIS TIME!

DID YOU SAY... LADYBUG?
5,000 YEARS AGO!!??
EVERYONE DOES HAVE A PAST THEY CAN LEARN FROM...
WELL, YOU DON'T LOOK A DAY OVER 3,000!
NOW YOU KNOW WHY I'M SO MUCH WISER THAN YOU!
HMPH!

OH, SACRED RA, GOD OF THE SUN, I, PHARAOH, OFFER TO THEE A PURE SOUL!

WHIRR
WHIRR
THIS SACRIFICE, FOR THE RETURN OF NEFERTITI!
I BOW TO YOU, AND PRESENT THIS GIFT WITH MY MUMMIES.
WE PRAY TO YOU FOR THE SAFE RETURN OF NEFERTITI!
AWAKEN, NEFERTITI! AWAKEN!
AH!

LADYBUUUUG!!!
WE'VE GOTTA SAVE HER BEFORE HE COMPLETES THE RITUAL!
OR ALYA WILL BE GONE, FOREVER!
WHAT SHOULD WE DO?
HOLD BACK THE MUMMIES WHILE I TAKE ON THE PHARAOH.
WHY DO *I* HAVE TO DEAL WITH THESE FREAKS WHILE *YOU* GET TO SLIP CALMLY ROUND BACK?!
BECAUSE I'M THE ONLY ONE WHO CAN CAPTURE HIS AKUMA... AND BECAUSE YOU'RE THE BRAVEST ONE OUT OF BOTH OF US!
I KNOW YOU REALLY DON'T THINK THAT... BUT I'LL PRETEND YOU DO!

LADYBUG!
GOTCHA!
BEST. DAY. EVER.
MY PRINCESS!
HOROS..

WWZZING
...GIVE ME YOUR WINGS!
PEEPS, YOU'VE JUST WITNESSED ANOTHER INSANE FEAT FROM LADYBUG!
THANKS FOR SAVING MY BUTT!
OH, UH, YOU'RE WELCOME! BUT IT'S NOT OVER YET, NOT UNTIL...
...NOT UNTIL LADYBUG DESTROYS THE PENDANT CONTAINING THE AKUMA AND TURNS EVERYTHING BACK TO NORMAL!

I PAY ATTENTION.
THE PENDANT! GOOD EYE!
THOOM
FWIP

UH... HELLO AGAIN!
GASP
NOOOO!!!
YOU'RE NOT GOING TO WIN THIS TIME, LADYBUG!
HELP ME, LADYBUG!
CRUSH THAT INSECT!!!

ALYA!
AAAAH!
FWOOSH

OOOOOOOOOOOOO
THAT ALL YOU GOT?
WHAT THE-?
OOOOOOOOOOOOOO

SNAG!
COUGH-
COUGH-
WOW, THOSE GUYS SURE ARE DUSTY!
CAT NOIR, THIS WAY!

SKREE
ZAP!
FWOOSH
FWISH
FWISH
YANK!
I'M COMING, ALYA!
HORUS...

...GIVE ME WINGS!
WZZING
WOAH!
AHHH!
SNAP!

CAT NOIR! THE PENDANT!
WHIR WHIR WHIR
THAT'S WHERE THE AKUMA IS!
THIS FIGHT ENDS NOW!

BOOOM
WOAAAH!
UGH...
LADYBUUUG! SAVE ME!

LUCKY...
FWIP FWIP FWIP
...CHARM!

A LADYBUG OUTFIT?!
THAT'S OUR LAST HOPE?
HMM...
LadyBug
DING!

THIS OFFERING ISN'T GOOD ENOUGH FOR NEFERTITI.
HEY!
THANKS A LOT!
SET ALYA FREE AND SACRIFICE *ME* INSTEAD!
WOULDN'T THAT BE THE SWEETEST REVENGE?
5,000 YEARS LATER!
AFTER ALL, I'M THE ONE WHO KEPT NEFERTITI FROM YOU ALL THESE YEARS!
IT'S TRUE THA YOU *WOULD* MA MUCH MORE PREC OFFERING THAN MORTAL...

HORUS, GIVE ME WINGS!
WWZZING
SERIOUSLY?
OOF!
EEK!
OW!
AH!
EXCUSE YOU!
I MAKE EXCELLENT SACRIFICE MATERIAL.

GASP
TAKE HER MIRACULOUS! THE EARRING!
YOU W
PHARAO
SWIPE!
WHAT IS THE MEANING OF THIS?!
YOU WANT MY MIRACULOUS?
GO GET IT!

GET IT!
TINK
WOOSH
JINGLE
JINGLE
A TOY?!
YOU TRICKED ME!
SMASH!

NO MORE EVIL-DOING FOR YOU, LITTLE AKUMA!
CLICK
SNAP!
TIME TO DE-EVILIZE!
GOTCHA!

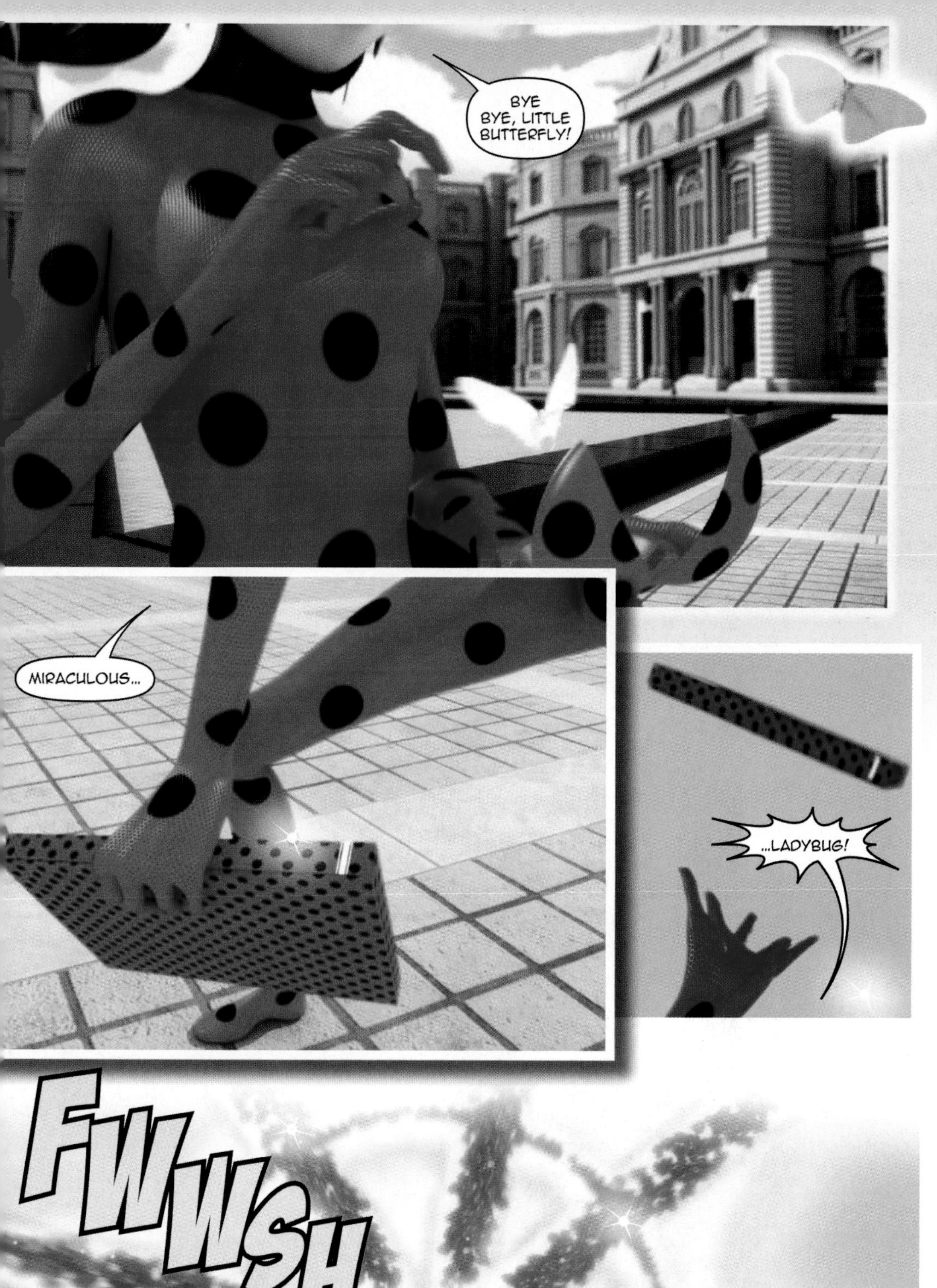
BYE BYE, LITTLE BUTTERFLY!
MIRACULOUS...
...LADYBUG!
FWWSH

FWOOSH

33

FWISH

33

GURGLE
GURGL

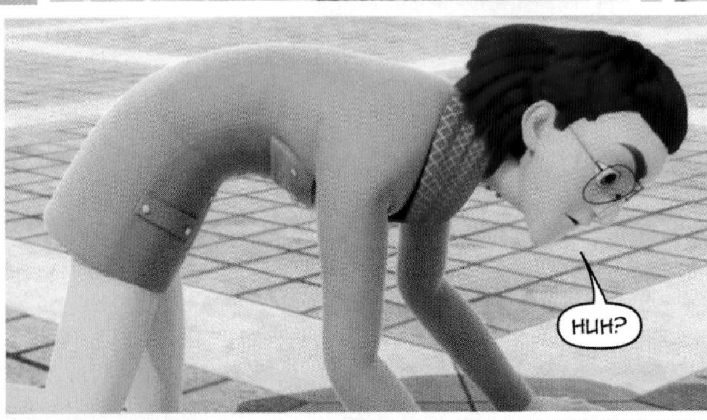
HUH?

WHAT HAPPENED?

THANKS, LADYBUG. BUT, UH... I STILL GOTTA ASK...
...HOW OLD ARE YOU, REALLY?
UM... MUCH OLDER THAN A HIGH SCHOOL STUDENT, THAT'S FOR SURE!
DON'T YOU WANT TO KNOW HOW OLD *I* AM?
IN A SEC, LOOKS LIKE I'LL BE ABLE TO TELL FOR MYSELF!
HUH?
UH-OH, MY RING!
BEEP BEEP BEEP
HEH HEH... GOTTA GO!

WHERE HAVE YOU BEEN?!

YOU WON'T BELIEVE THIS!

I GOT MUMMIFIED!

WHAT!? YOU WERE ALMOST... SACRIFICED?!?
HOPE YOU WEREN'T ONE OF THE ONES TRYING TO SWAP ME FOR NEFERTITI. CREEPY!

IF IT HADN'T BEEN FOR YOU, I'D NEVER HAVE FOUND OUT THAT LADYBUG IS AT LEAST 5,000 YEARS OLD!
HEY! WHAT ARE FRIENDS FOR?

I STILL DON'T GET IT, THOUGH... WHAT WAS SHE DOING WITH THAT 10TH GRADE HISTORY TEXTBOOK?

UH... SHE...

...SHE PROBABLY HAD TO FIND OUT WHAT'S BEEN GOING ON FOR THE PAST 50 CENTURIES!

HA! YOU'RE PROBABLY RIGHT. IT'S TOUGH STAYING IN THE LOOP!

HEYYY! LADYBUG'S TEXTBOOK!

T'S
ONE!

GIGGLE

YOU MIGHT HAVE GOTTEN AWAY THIS TIME, BUT I ASSURE YOU, LADYBUG, SOMEDAY, WHEREVER YOU ARE, I *WILL* HAVE YOUR MIRACULOUS, AND YOU'LL BE NOTHING.
NOTHING AT ALL!

I DON'T GET IT.
I KNOW I'M NOT 5,000 YEARS OLD, SO...
...WHO EXACTLY **WAS** THAT LADYBUG IN THE PAPYRUS?
KWAMIS LIKE ME AND SUPERHEROES LIKE YOU HAVE ALWAYS EXISTED!
SO THAT WASN'T YOU ON THE PAPYRUS, EITHER?
WHAT DO YOU THINK?
YOU DON'T LOOK 5,000 YEARS OLD...
WELL, I'M NOT.... I'M OLDER THAN THAT!
I'M THE KWAMI WHO HAS WATCHED OVER EVERY SINGLE LADYBUG, SINCE THE VERY BEGINNING!
YOU MUST HAVE KNOWN MUCH LESS KLUTZY LADYBUGS THAN ME, RIGHT?
EVERY LADYBUG IS DIFFERENT.
MARINETTE. YOU **ARE** DIFFERENT, BUT DIFFERENT AS IN SURPRISING, UNPREDICTABLE AND ENDEARING.
AND VERY TALENTED! YOU LEARN FAST!
REMEMBER, YOU HAVE THAT HISTORY TEST TOMORROW!
NOW, YOU BETTER GET TO SLEEP.
OH YEAH... GOOD THING IT'S ON ANCIENT EGYPT!

HOW ABOUT INVITING HIM TO A MOVIE, THEN?

RIGHT TIKKI, CAN YOU IMAGINE THAT CONVERSATION?

opycat

ted by: Thomas Astruc
cs adaptation by: Nicole D'Andria
ten by: Sébastien Thibaudeau
Pascal Boutboul
rranged by: Cheryl Black
red by: Justin Birch

"WOULD YOU LIKE TO-"

"-GAH! WA! WUH!"

I CAN'T HELP IT.

EVERY TIME I SEE HIM, I GET ALL CLAMMY AND FEEL LIKE FAINTING!
SO... BASICALLY, THE ONLY WAY YOU CAN HAVE A NORMAL CONVERSATION WITH HIM IS IF YOU'RE BLINDFOLDED!
PRETTY MUCH!
THERE *IS* A VERY SIMPLE SOLUTION, MARINE IT'S CALLED A CELL PHONE! YO JUST NEED HIS NUMBER.
I KNOW WHO'LL HAVE ADRIEN'S NUMBER!
Alya +33636768
CLICK!
RING RING! RING RING!

LOOK, E ALL KNOW ROV'S NOT YOUR AG, SO JUST TICK TO THIS SCRIPT...
BUT ALL THE TEACHERS SAY I DON'T SOUND NATURAL WHEN I READ!
THEN MEMORIZE IT!
IT'S PRETTY SIMPLE. YOU CAN DO THIS!
JUST DON'T IMPROVISE, GOT IT?
I...

FORGET IT! THIS IS NEVER GONNA WORK!
CLICK!
TOO LATE, IT'S DIALING!
GASP
HEY!

EEEK!
THIS IS ADRIEN'S VOICEMAIL. LEAVE A MESSAGE!
ITS GONE TO VOICEMAIL!
LEAVE A MESSAGE. DON'T IMPROV!
HELLO... UH, ADRIEN'S VOICEMAIL...
UGH...
UM... THIS IS MARINETTE... WHO... UH... HAS A MESSAGE... FOR YOU, OF COURSE... CUZ IT'S... UH, YOUR PHONE.
SO... UM... HEH HEH...

CALL-ME-BYE-SEE-YA-LATER!

SIGH

WHAT?

WHAT DID YOU EXPECT ME TO SAY?!

"HEY, HOT STUFF! THIS IS MARINETTE!"
"I'D ASK YOU ON A DATE TO A MOVIE, BUT I'VE GOT SUCH A CRAZY CRUSH ON YOU-"
"-THAT THE ONLY WAY I CAN TALK TO YOU WITHOUT FOAMING AT THE MOUTH IS OVER THIS STUPID PHONE."
"PRETTY RIDICULOUS, RIIIIGHT?"
HM?
Adrien
IF YOU WISH TO HEAR YOUR MESSAGE AGAIN, PRESS 1; IF YOU WISH TO ERASE YOUR MESSAGE, PRESS 2.
GASP
HIT 2!!! HIT 2!!!
CLICK!
MESSAGE SAVED. GOODBYE.

NOOOOOOOOO!!!
IT'S NOT AS BAD AS YOU THINK.
...OK, IT'S BAD. BUT YOU WERE GONNA HAVE TO TELL HIM ONE OF THESE DAYS... SOME WAY OR ANOTHER.
THINK OF IT THIS WAY: NO MORE SECRETS!
THE VOICEMAIL RECORDED MY WHOLE CONVERSATION.
BIG DEAL!
I CALLED HIM "HOT STUFF."
HE CAN NOT BE ALLOWED TO HEAR THAT MESSAGE, ALYA! IF HE DOES, I'LL DIE OF SHAME!

OKAY, OKAY! I GOT AN IDEA.
IF ADRIEN'S PHONE WENT TO VOICEMAIL, IT MEANS THE DUDE'S BUSY... WHICH ALSO MEANS YOU CAN GET TO IT BEFORE HE DOES!
HMM... I WONDER WHERE HE'D BE...
OF COURSE! HE'S GOT FENCING CLUB AFTER SCHOOL... THAT'S WHY HE DIDN'T PICK UP!
IT ENDS IN EXACTLY 22 AND A HALF MINUTES!
YOU ARE SERIOUSLY INSANE. YOU KNOW THAT, RIGHT?
⋟GIGGLE⋞
SAINT VALENTIN
ESCRIME
SORTIE AVEC SES AMIS.
BASKET TOUJOURS
SHOOTING PHOTO (PARC)

HEE HEE. YOU HAVE ONE NEW MESSAGE...
BURP
MOVE PLEASE, SO I CAN CHECK MY VOICEMAIL.
HMM, DON'T RECOGNIZE THIS NUMBER.
Inconnu +33636768
Nino +33689562
Père +33678424
Chloé
OH NO, NOW WE'RE LATE! TIME TO TRANSFORM, PLAGG!
TING

HEY EVERYBODY!
THEY'RE UNVEILING LADYBUG AND CAT NOIR SCULPTURES TODAY!
I TOTALLY SPACED!
ME TOO!
UH, YOU NEVER MENTIONED GOING TO THE UNVEILING BEFORE...?
I'M NOT! I MEAN, I AM. UH... I MEAN... I FORGOT???
LISTEN, ABOUT ADRIEN'S CELL PHONE... WHAT IF WE GO RIGHT AFTER?
IF WE WAIT 'TIL AFTER THE CEREMONY, ADRIEN'S FENCING TRAINING WILL BE OVER, AND HE'LL HAVE HIS PHONE BACK BY THEN!
BONBONS
CONFISERIE TRADITIONNELLE
SHOOT! I GOTTA COVER THIS EVENT FOR THE LADYBLOG. I'M SORRY MARINETTE...
DON'T SWEAT IT. I CAN MANAGE! ...I THINK.
YOU SURE?
YES, YES, I'M SURE!
COOL. GOOD LUCK... AND STAY OUTTA TROUBLE. ***AND DON'T IMPROV!***

WOOHOO!
HOORAY!
SNAP! SNAP!
EXCUSE ME CAT NOIR, BUT... LADYBUG'S NOT HERE.
DON'T WORRY ABOUT LADYBUG, I'M SURE SHE'LL BE HERE ANY MINUTE. I CAN HANDLE THIS SITUATION ALONE FOR NOW. I'M THE ONE IN CHARGE ANYWAY, YOU KNOW!
IT'S JUST THAT... I WANTED TO ASK HER TO AUTOGRAPH THIS PHOTO. SHE'S AMAZING!

OH BOY...
AAAAH! WHICH ONE'S HIS?!
IF YOU CALL HIM, YOU'LL MAKE HIS PHONE RING!
RING RING!
RING RING!
RING RING! RING RING!

IT'S ONLY PROPER FOR PARIS TO PAY HOMAGE TO THOSE WHO PROTECT US FROM EVIL...
...LADYBUG AND CAT NOIR!
OOOOOH!
SIGH

HERE IT IS!
RING RING! RING RING!
URGH...
RING RING! RING RING!
AAAAH! IT'S LOCKED!
ZWOOP!
TIKKI?

TADA!
TIKKI, YOU'RE A LIFE-SAVER!

THESE STATUES ARE AMAZING! ONE THING'S SLIGHTLY OFF, THOUGH...
...I'M ACTUALLY TALLER THAN LADYBUG.
LADYBUG DIDN'T SHOW UP. I JUST WANTED TO EXPRESS MY ADORATION FOR HER... LET HER KNOW THAT EVERYTHING I HAD WENT INTO HER STATUE.
I'M SURE IF SHE JUST TOOK A LITTLE TIME TO GET TO KNOW ME, SHE WOULD SEE HOW MUCH WE HAVE IN COMMON— OUR DEVOTION TO THE THINGS WE LOVE!
HEY, DON'T MEAN TO BURST YOUR BUBBLE, BUT YOU KNOW, LADYBUG AND ME, WE'RE A THING. YOU KNOW?
REALLY?
YEAH, WE'RE LIKE THIS!
...REALLY?
GRRR... WHAT DOES LADYBUG SEE IN HIM?!?

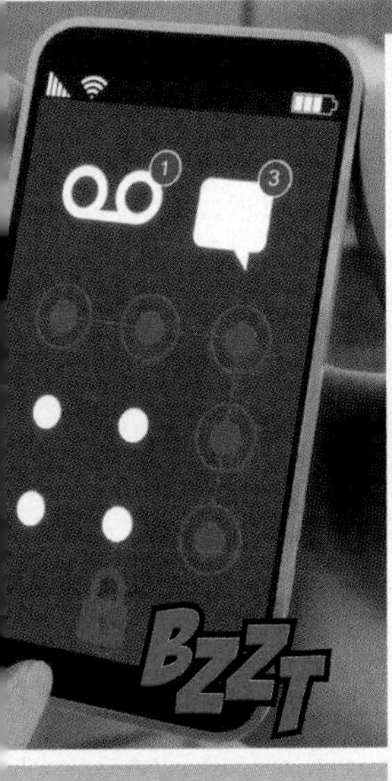
BZZT

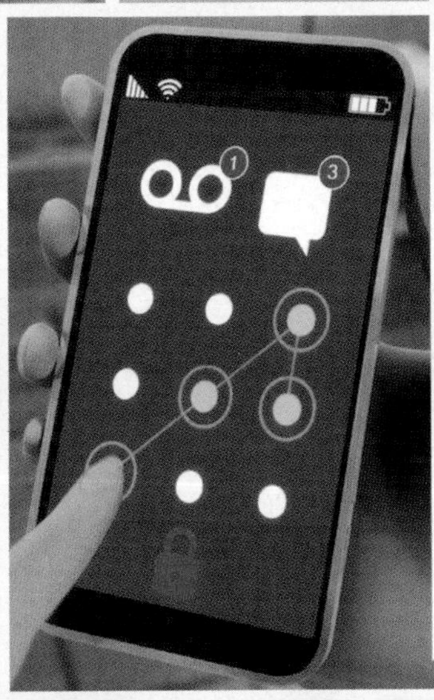

BZZT

THEY'RE COMING! FORGET THE PHONE!

I HAVEN'T ERASED THE MESSAGE YET!

BZZT

WHEW THAT WAS ROUGH!

A "THING," HUH? YOU DON'T EVEN TAKE *LOVE* SERIOUSLY.
CALLING IT A "THING."
Incroyable !!

YOU DON'T DESERVE HER!
I DO!!!
SLAM!
I DO...

DISAPPOINTED BY LADYBUG AND JEALOUS OF CAT NOIR. THE PERFECT FORMULA...
...FOR DISASTER!
WWZZING
FLY AWAY MY LITTLE AKUMA AND EVILIZE HIM!

FWWSH
HELLO, COPYCAT.
I'M HAWK MOTH. ONCE YOU GET RID OF CAT NOIR, YOU CAN TAKE HIS PLACE. AND LADYBUG WILL BE YOURS FOREVER!
THE VE
THOUGHT
MAKES
PURR
HISSSS
HISSSSSS

WHAT IF HE TRACKS IT? HE'LL FIGURE OUT I STOLE IT!
I'LL BE ARRESTED FOR GRAND THEFT!
I'LL SPEND THE REST OF MY LIFE IN JAIL!
AND WORSE...
...I'LL NEVER GET TO GO TO THE MOVIES WITH ADRIEN!
MARINETTE... YOU REALLY NEED TO GET YOUR PRIORITIES IN ORDER!
I KNOW. SOME DAYS IT FEELS IMPOSSIBLE TO BALANCE BEING MARINETTE AND BEING LADYBUG!
HEY! THIS IS ADRIEN'S VOICEMAIL. LEAVE A MESSAGE!
HMM, IT MUST STILL BE AT THE GYM!

WHOA!
IS THAT-?

SNAP!
SO COOL!
SNAP!

DON'T MIND ME!

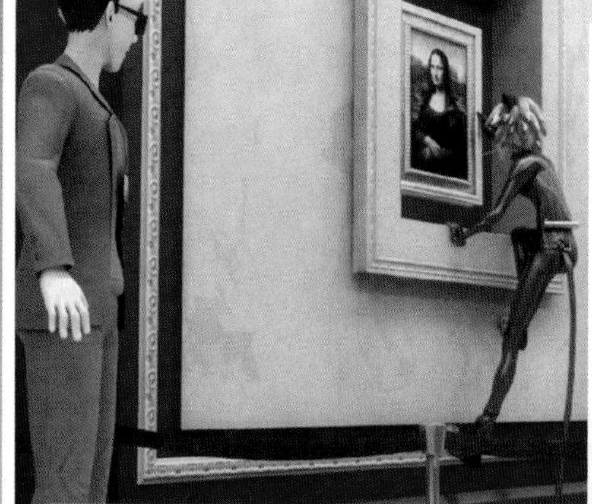

JUST STEALING THIS PAINTING. GO ABOUT YOUR BUSINESS!
WEE-OOOO

WEE-OOOO
HEY!

WEE-OOOO

HAVE A NICE TRIP!

SEE YOU NEXT NEVER!
WEE-OOOO

UGH...

GASP
GASP

WEE-OOOO
REC
THIS PAINTING IS THE CAT'S MEOW!

AND IN SOME ASTONISHING NEWS: THERE'S BEEN A SPECTACULAR THEFT AT THE LOUVRE!
HUH?
AMATEUR VIDEO SHOWED WITHOUT A SHADOW OF A DOUBT THAT THE THIEF IS NONE OTHER THAN THE FAMOUS HERO, CAT NOIR!
THIS PAINTING IS THE CAT'S MEOW!
"CAT" MEOW
NOT ONLY IS THAT PERSON A FAKE, HE'S A TERRIBLE FAKE!
AND NOW, GOOD NEWS FOR LETTUCE LOVERS...

UGH. OF
COURSE ADRIEN
OULD OWN ONE
F THESE SUPER-
ENSIVE HIGH-TECH
SMARTPHONES.
POKE
I CAN'T EVEN FIGURE OUT HOW TO WORK THIS THING!
POKE POKE
MAYBE IT WOULD HELP IF YOU TOOK OFF THOSE SILLY MITTENS?
AND RISK LEAVING FINGERPRINTS? NO WAY!
RING RING!
PROBLEM FIXED?

ALMOST. I HAVE''T ERASED THE MESSAGE YET... BUT I'M WORKING ON IT AS WE SPEAK!
NO WAY, YOU PALMED PHONE?!
YES- NO- ERRR... I MEAN, I WAS PLANNING TO GIVE IT BACK!
ACTUALLY, WHERE ARE YOU? I COULD USE SOME HELP!
NO CAN DO!
I'M WAITING FOR ADDITIONAL DEETS AT THE LOUVRE ON THE CAT NOIR ROBBERY...
WHAT?! SOMEBODY ROBBED CAT NOIR?
NO GIRL! DIDN'T YOU HEAR?
CAT NOIR CAME IN AND STOLE THE MONA LISA! IN BROAD DAYLIGHT!
LADYBUG'S GONNA TURN UP FOR SURE, AND I DO **NOT** WANNA MISS IT. JUST CHILL AND I'LL BE OVER LATER.
'KAY.
CAT NOIR IS A LOT OF THINGS BUT HE'S NO THIEF!

TIME TO TRANSFORM!
TIKKI, SPOTS ON!
TING
FWWSH
SWISH

CAT NOIR SPOTTED!
WOAH, EASY TIGERS! YOU'VE GOT THE WRONG CAT! THAT THIEF'S AN IMPOSTOR. I'M THE REAL CAT NOIR!
LEMME CHECK OUT WHERE THE ROBBERY TOOK PLACE. I HAVE A KNACK FOR FINDING CLUES.
POLICE
POLICE
YOU KNOW, ANIMAL INSTINCTS.
POLICE
OF COURSE, COME WITH ME. THANKS FOR YOUR HELP, CAT NOIR.

HMM...
OH!
HE MUST HAVE LEFT THIS BEHIND.
POLICE
CLICK!
SWOOSH
SLAM!

HEY! *I'M* THE REAL CAT NOIR!
I'M WAAAY SLICKER THAN THAT GUY!
KITTY'S IN THE SLAMMER. I REPEAT, KITTY'S IN THE SLAMMER!
POLICE
MISTER MAYOR, THIS IS RIDICULOUS!
I'M SURE THERE'S A SIMPLE EXPLANATION.

KITTY'S IN THE SLAMMER, LADYBUG!
DON'T THINK YOU'RE GONNA KEEP HIM THERE-
NOW, NOW!
LEAVE IT TO THE EXPERTS, LADYBUG.
WE'VE GOT IT UNDER CONTROL.

POLICE
CAT NOIR'S GETTING AWAY!

WHAT?!

GASP

UGH...

WELL, IF HE'S SO INNOCENT, THEN WHY IS HE RUNNING AWAY?

WELL, IF YOU WERE WRONGLY IMPRISONED, WOULDN'T YOU RUN?

HUFF HUFF
LADYBUG, WHERE ARE YOU?

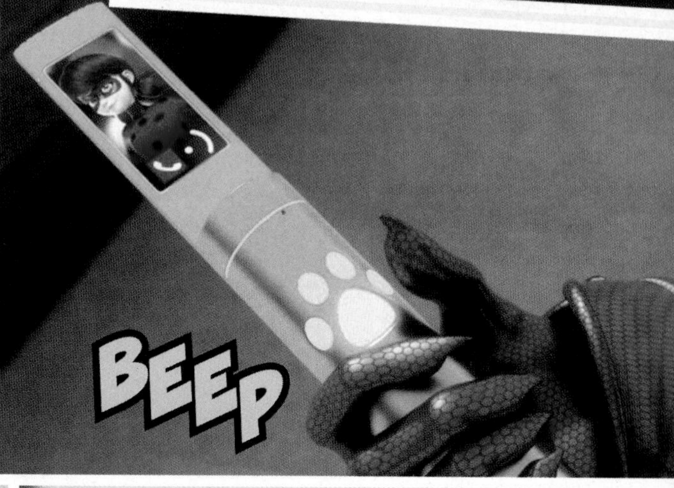
BEEP

BEEP BEEP
REQUESTING ASSISTANCE. I REPEAT, REQUESTING ASSISTANCE. WE ARE...
CAT NOIR? WHAT'S GOING ON?!
YOU KNOW I'M INNOCENT, DON'T YOU, BUGABOO?
STOP PLAYING AROUND AND CALLING ME BUGABOO! THIS IS REALLY SERIOUS!
I'M GONNA FIND THE REAL CULPRIT AND SAVE MY TAIL! I'LL GET BACK TO YOU.
WHUP WHUP WHIP

POLICE
WHUP WHUP WHIP
GIVE YOURSELF UP, CAT NOIR!

GASP

WEE-OOOO
WEE-OOOO
WEE-OOOO
WEE-OOOO
WEE-OOOO
IF YOU WANT MY OPINION, I'D SAY THE THIEF WAS AKUMATIZED!
THAT MUCH I
SEE THAT LOLLIPOP STICK?
THE SCULPTOR!
HOW DID I NOT SEE THAT JEALOUSY COMING A MILE AWAY?

L'ATELIER
GOTCHA, COPYCAT.
WHERE IS HE?
BEEP BEEP
CLICK!
I'VE FOUND HIS DEN!

WHO?

MY COPYCAT!

I'M NOT GETTING YOU...?

IF YOU'D BEEN THERE THIS MORNING, YOU'D KNOW WHAT I WAS TALKING ABOUT.
WELL, TELL ME WHERE YOU ARE!
NO! THIS IS BETWEEN ME AND HIM.
I GOT MYSELF INTO THIS MESS.
SO NOW I'M GONNA GET MYSELF OUT OF IT!
CLICK!
CAT? CAT??!!
UGH...
CLICK!
BEEP
BEEP
FINE, I'LL JUST FIND YOU MYSELF!

"CAT'S IN THE BAG?"
Le Chat est dans le Sac!
CLICK!
FWOOSH
HEY!
CLICK! CLICK!

JINGLE
YOU REALLY THINK THIS WILL WORK? HA!

CATACLYSM!
CRUNCH

AH!

FWWSH

HEH HEH.

I
N'T GET WHAT
YBUG SEES IN
—A FOOL WHO
EASILY FALLS
TO MY TRAP!
HMPF! SAYS THE GUY WITH WORSE PUNS THAN ME!

GASP
MY STAFF!

LOOKING FOR THIS?

WHICH ONE SHOULD I PICK UP?

MY ONE, OR...
BEEP BEEP
...MY ONE?!
LADYBUG, HURRY UP! I'VE CAUGHT THE IMPOSTER AT THEO BARBEAU'S WORKSHOP!
I'LL BE THERE IN THIRTY SECONDS!
DON'T COME HERE, LADYBUG! IT'S A TRAP!
TOO LATE, CAT! LADYBUG'S ON HER WAY, WHICH WAS MY PLAN ALL ALONG.

STOP THIS ALL TALK AND ME CAT NOIR'S IRACULOUS!

ZIP!

YAAH!

HUNK

OOF...
THUD!

HA! TOO EASY.
GASP
GASP
THERE YOU ARE!
CAT NOIR!

HE REALLY LOOKS LIKE YOU!
THAT'S BECAUSE *I AM ME!*
HEH. SUUURE YOU ARE.
WHERE'S HIS AKUMA?
INSIDE HIS RING, OF COURSE.
GRAB IT.
LADYBUG'S DOING ALL THE WORK FOR US. WHAT SWEET IRONY!

HE EVEN HAS THE SAME POWERS AS YOU?!

BEEP
BEEP
BEEP

SIMPLY AMAZING, ISN'T IT?

IF YOU DON'T BELIEVE I'M THE REAL CAT NOIR, ASK HIM ABOUT OUR LOVE FOR EACH OTHER.
HUH?
HAVE I EVER LIED TO YOU, *BUGABOO?*

BUGABOO?

I HOPE YOU DIDN'T TELL HIM ABOUT US?
WHASSAT?

THAT WE'RE... YOU KNOW!

WE MADE A SECRET PROMISE?
OH, YES, OF COURSE!
WE NEVER MADE A PROMISE... COPYCAT!
WHAT?
NO!
I LOVE YOU, LADYBUG!
I'M WAY BETTER THAN THIS MANGY ALLEY CAT!
SORRY, BUT LIARS ARE LOSERS!

LET'S WRAP THIS UP!
LUCKY...
FWIP FWIP FWIP FWIP
...CHARM!
FWWSH

A SPOON? WHAT AM I SUPPOSED TO DO WITH THIS?!

HERE HE COMES!
WAIT A MINUTE, I HAVE AN IDEA!
HYAAAH!
SWISH

SNAP
CRACKLE
CRACKLE
EXCELLENT JOB, M'LADY!
WHERE'S HIS AKUMA?
PHOTO IN HIS POCKET.
BEEP
BEEP
BEEP
WE'RE GONNA HAVE TO MAKE IT SNAPPY!

BACK OFF!
CLANG!
HE'S PRETTY GOOD.
DON'T NEED TO RUB IT IN.
I TOLD YOU I WAS BETTER THAN HIM!
FWOOSH
SNAG!

NO!
BUT I'M BETTER THA
BOTH OF YOU!
CAT NOIR!
CATCH!
THANKS, BUGABOO!
ARGH!

I'LL WIPE THAT SMIRK OFF YOUR FACE!
YOU CAN TRY!
SNAG

HEY, IT'S ME!

HE'S LYING! ***I'M*** THE REAL ONE!

...OOPS?
AAARGH! NOW YOU'RE BOTH ANNOYING ME TO PIECES!
SHOW ME YOUR RING! HOW MANY PADS DO YOU HAVE LEFT?
BEEP BEEP BEEP
BEEP
BEEP
BEEP BEEP
GRR...

HMM...
DING!
DING!
DING!
DING!

THAT'S IT!

SCRRRTCH

SCR
SCRTC

PERFECT.

TIME TO GO AKUMA FISHING!

COME AND GET ME, KITTY!
ARGH!
?
WINK
SWISH
SWOOSH

SNAG
GET AWAY FROM THERE!
ZIP!

WOAAAH!
SWOOSH
I'LL TAKE THAT PHOTO, THANK YOU!
RIIIP!
CLICK

NO MORE EVIL-DOING FOR YOU, LITTLE AKUMA!
TIME TO DE-EVILIZE!
SNAP!
GOTCHA!
CLICK
BYE BYE, LITTLE BUTTERFLY.
MIRACULOUS...
...LADYBUG!

WWSH
SWOOSH

WOOSH

Incroyable !!

BETTER HELP THE FELLOW OUT. HIS CRUSH JUST GOT CRUSHED.
UGH...
THAT MAKES TWO OF US...
LADYBUG?!
I'M SORRY I COULDN'T MAKE IT THIS MORNING, THEO.

CAN YOU AUTOGRAPH IT FOR ME?
OF COURSE I CAN!
YOU'VE GOT SOME REAL ARTISTRY HERE. YOU REALLY CAPTURED MY ESSENCE.
Incroyable !!
Et tamen in busda taneque pecun modut est neque nonor imper ned libiding gen epular religuard on quas undant
THANK YOU, LADYBUG! AND DON'T WORRY... I KNOW ABOUT YOU AND CAT NOIR. IT'S OKAY.
HUH?

IF YOU WISH TO HEAR YOUR MESSAGE AGAIN, PRESS 1.

IF YOU WISH TO ERASE YOUR MESSAGE, PRESS 2.

CLICK!

YOU KNOW WHAT? I'M GONNA TELL HIM I FOUND HIS PHONE.

THAT'D BE A GOOD WAY TO START UP A CONVERSATION, WOULDN'T IT? THEN I'LL INVITE HIM TO THE MOVIES.

THAT'S MY GIRL

MAYBE YOU DROPPED IT SOMEWHERE?
WELL, IF I DID, THEN WHOEVER HAS IT FOUND IT IN THE BOYS' LOCKER ROOM.
I WAS CHECKING MY VOICEMAIL IN THERE DURING FENCING PRACTICE.

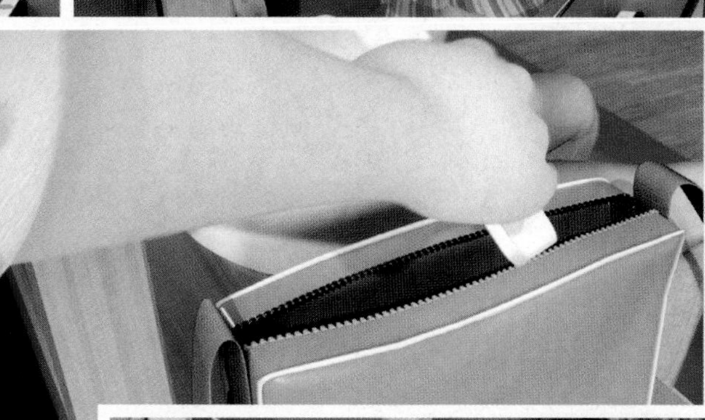

HUH? WHAT IN THE...?

I ALREADY LOOKED IN HERE A THOUSAND TIMES!
YOU NEED SOME TIME OFF. HEY, I KNOW, LET'S GO TO THE MOVIES TONIGHT.
HEY, DUDES, MIND IF A FEW FRIENDS TAG ALONG?
SURE THING!
GIGGLE
SOUNDS FUN.
WOOHOO!!!

Timebreaker
Created by: Thomas Astruc
Comics adaptation by: Nicole D'Andria
Written by: Sébastien Thibaudeau
Michaël Delachenal
Art arranged by: Cheryl Black
Lettered by: Justin Birch
WELL?
WITH OR WITHOUT?
UH... WITH?
YOU'RE SURE IT'S NOT BETTER WITHOUT?
EITHER Y YOU LOOK PERFECT, MOM.
IT'S NOT EVERY DAY THAT YOU CELEBRATE YOUR 20TH WEDDING ANNIVERSARY!
WE NEED TO GET GOING, HONEY.

YOU'RE GOING TO BE LATE!
NOW DON'T FORGET-
-MRS. CHAMACK WILL BE COMING BY TO PICK UP THE EIFFEL TOWER CAKE IN 30 MINUTES. I'M DEPENDING ON YOU!
YEAH, YEAH. NO SWEAT.
PIECE OF CAKE!

OH!
THEY'RE MARINETTE'S PARENTS.
YOU KNOW, ONE OF THE CHICKS I HANG OUT WITH?
YES, I REMEMBER. THEY MAKE THE BEST BREAD IN THE WHOLE OF PARIS.
COULDN'T YOU HAVE MADE MORE OF AN EFFORT TO DRESS NICELY?
WHAT D'YOU MEAN?

I TOOK MY

BUT THIS IS A *SPECIAL* DAY.

WELL, IT'S ONLY A BIRTHDAY...

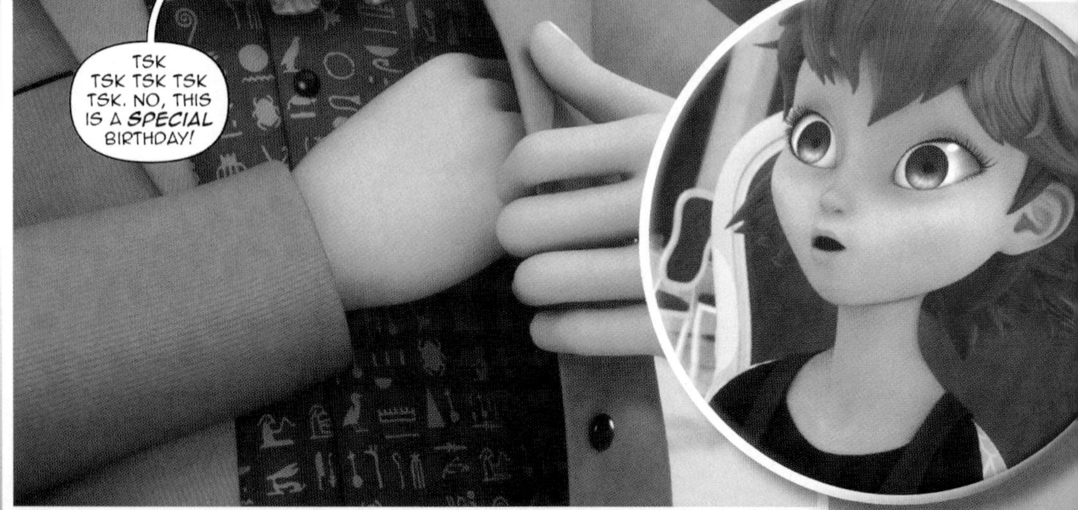
TSK TSK TSK TSK TSK. NO, THIS IS A *SPECIAL* BIRTHDAY!

THIS FAMILY HEIRLOOM WAS MADE BY ONE OF OUR ANCESTORS MANY, MANY YEARS AGO.
IT'S EN PASSED OWN FROM GENERATION THE NEXT, THEIR 15TH BIRTHDAY.
AND TODAY, IT'S YOUR TURN TO INHERIT IT!
IT'S PRETTY SWEET, DAD. BUT I'VE ALREADY GOT A WATCH SYNCHED UP TO MY SMARTPHONE.

BUT SOMETIMES THERE'S MORE TO THINGS THAN MEETS THE EYE.
LET'S JUST SAY OUR ANCESTOR WAS...
CLICK
WEE-OOP
WEE-OOP

FWOOSH

WHOA!
OF COURSE...
...I'D UNDERSTAND IF YOU'D RATHER ME BUY YOU A NEW PAIR OF ROLLERBLADES...
CLICK
NO, DAD!
I'M STOKED TO HAVE IT! IT'S AWESOME! THANK YOU!

RIIING!
ARE YOUR FRIENDS WAITING?
YEAH, BUT I DON'T WANNA BAIL ON YOU. IT'S COOL.
NO, NO, GO AHEAD!
NOW, TAKE GOOD CARE OF IT.
NO PROB, DAD!

C'MON MARINETTE! YOU CAN DO IT!
JUST REMEMBER THE FORMULA! THINK, MARINETTE! THINK!
I MIGHT BE ABLE TO IF YOU WEREN'T DISTRACTING ME SO MUCH WITH YOUR ENCOURAGING WORDS!
RING!
GIGGLE
CLICK
HEY, ALYA! WASSUP? THE WHAT?
THE BET BETWEEN ALIX AND KIM?!?! NO, OF COURSE I DIDN'T FORGET!

I ALREADY MADE THE BANNER FOR IT! I KNOW EVERYONE'S COUNTING ON ME.
IN FIVE MINUTES? NO SWEAT, I'M ON MY WAY ALREADY! BE RIGHT THERE...
EEEE!
BUT MARINETTE!
YOU HAV TO WAIT F MRS. CHAM TO PICK HER CAK
GAAH!

TIKKI, SPOTS ON!
THWOOM
HEY EVERYBODY!

YOU ALL PICKED THE WRONG SIDE TO CHEER ON!
LOOKS LIKE ALIX ISN'T EVEN SHOWING UP.
PROBABLY TOO CHICKEN TO RACE AN EXTREME ATHLETE LIKE ME!
SPOKE TOO SOON, KIM!
YOUR RIDICULOUS BETS ARE OVER.
I'M GONNA LEAVE YOU IN THE DUST, MEATHEAD!
YOU'RE NO MATCH FOR ME!

MY NECK IS BIGGER THAN YOUR THIGH!
HA HA.
IS THAT A GOOD THING?
GIGGLE
LET'S REVIEW THE OFFICIAL RULES: TWO LAPS AROUND THE FOUNTAINS, APPROXIMATELY 500 YARDS.
THE FIRST ONE OVER THE LINE IS DECLARED THE VICTOR.
IF KIM RIUMPHS, ALIX RELINQUISH HER OLLERBLADES TO HIM.
IF ALIX TRIUMPHS, KIM WILL BE PROHIBITED FROM MAKING ANOTHER DARE FOR THE REST OF THE SCHOOL YEAR!

YEAH, THAT'S RIGHT!
NO MORE DARES!
WE'RE THROUGH WITH ALL OF THOSE STUPID DARES!

ON YOUR MARKS...

...GET SET...

HOLD UP!
OOF!

FORFEITING ALREADY?

HOLD ONTO THIS FOR ME, WILL YA, ALYA?
I DO WANNA IT DURIN RAC

HOLD ON GIRL, I CAN'T! I GOTTA-
GUARD IT WITH YOUR LIFE. IT'S A FAMILY HEIRLOOM!
BUT-
-AND SHE'S GONE.
MARINETTE, TAKE THIS!
I GOTTA RECORD THE RACE FOR MY BLOG!
ON YOUR MARKS, GET SET...

...GO!!!
YAAY!
BUT... SHE ASKED YOU TO HOLD IT. I GOTTA HOLD UP THE BANNER!
EEK!
NO!

NEED ANY HELP?
UH... YEP, THANKS.
GOTTA BE CAREFUL!
EVEN IF YOU ARE AMAZING....
?
GASP
...AT...
HOLDING THINGS...
IN YOUR HANDS!
WOOHOO!

FASTER!
GO ALIX!
YOU'RE GONNA WIN ALIX!

LAST LAP!

AMAZING AT HOLDING THINGS?

ADRIKINS!

ATCHA
THERE?
SOME SUPER OLD CASE OR SOMETHING?
CAREFUL, IT'S ALIX'S!
IF IT'S ALIX'S, IT'S PROBABLY WORTHLESS!
GIVE IT BACK TO ADRIEN, CHLOÉ!
CLICK
GASP

SQUEAK!
GO ALIX!
OOPS...
THE WATCH!

SMASH!

GASP

HUFF
HUFF
HUFF
HUFF
HUFF
I CALL A REMATCH! THAT FALSE START BACK THERE THREW ME OFF!

HMPH. IN YOUR DREAMS, MEATHEAD!

GASP

DID YOU DO THIS?!

UH... I...

...HAD TO VIDEOTAPE THE RACE, SO I GAVE IT TO MARINETTE.

BUT SHE HAD TO HOLD THE BANNER SO SHE GAVE IT TO ADRIEN, THEN CHLOÉ SNATCHED IT FROM HIM AND DROPPED IT.

AND THEN YOU SKATED OVER IT.
MY OLD MAN GAVE THIS TO ME FOR MY BIRTHDAY.
THIS WATCH IS TOTALLY A FAMILY HEIRLOOM!
IT WAS AN ACCIDENT!
I TOTALLY HAD NOTHING TO DO WITH THIS.
YOU'RE ALL TO BLAME!!!

SUCH DISAPPOINTMENT, FRUSTRATION, AND NEGATIVITY.
OH, HOW IT FILLS MY HEART WITH EXHILARATION!

WWZZING
FLY AWAY, MY LITTLE AKUMA, AND EVILIZE HER!

KNOCK
KNOCK
CONFISERIE
BOULANGERIE
IT'S MRS. CHAMACK.
RING RING!
HELLO? YES, I... I KNOW YOU NEED YOUR CAKE RIGHT AWAY.
MY DAUGHTER'S HOME. SHE MUST BE UPSTAIRS... I'LL PHONE HER IMMEDIATELY!
CLICK

RING RING!
Papa
UH-OH... THIS CAN'T BE GOOD.
HELLO, DAD?
FWWSH
TIMEBREAKER, I AM HAWK MOTH.
I'M GRANTING YOU THE POWER TO RETALIATE AGAINST THE PEOPLE WHO'VE WRONGED YOU AND TO GO BACK IN TIME TO RESTORE THE FUTURE.
BUT YOU MUST DO ME A FAVOR IN RETURN, WHEN THE TIME IS RIGHT...
YOU GOT IT,

SCREECH
UH... I... I GOTTA GO, DAD!
CAN'T KEEP MRS. CHAMACK WAITING!
SHE WAS LISTENING TO MUSIC.

GASP
HEH HEH. TIME FOR SOME REVENGE.
RUN!

OH PLEASE, YOU'RE NOWHERE NEAR FAST ENOUGH!

ZWICK
STOP, ALIX! WHAT'RE YOU DOING?!?
THE NAME'S TIMEBREAKER NOW.

AND I'M GOING TO GO BACK IN TIME AND SAVE MY WATCH, USING ALL OF YOU PUNKS TO DO IT!
GO BACK IN TIME?! WHAT DID YOU DO TO KIM? WHY IS HE FADING AWAY?!

I NEEDED HIS ENERGY.
BESIDES, THE DUDE WAS A PAIN ANYWAY, WITH ALL THOSE BETS!
HE DESERVES TO DISAPPEAR FOREVER... AND SO DO YOU!
ALIX NO!
SORRY, ALIX.

OH, WHOOPS!
UGH!
GRRR... WHERE...?
WE GOTTA TRANSFORM.
NOW!

TIKKI, SPOTS ON!
TIN
FWWSH
SWISH

FWISH
FWOOSH
YEE-OUCH!
OOF...
YOU...
TIME OUT, TIMEBREAKER!

PLEASE, HELP ME UP! I'M MESSED UP. PLEASE... PLEASE...
NOOO!
HA HA HA HA HA!
ZWICK
GASP
SWEET ROSE. ALWAYS THINKING OF OTHERS BEFORE YOURSELF!
BLEEP BLEEP
ONE MINUTE
I GOTTA DESTROY HER AKUMA BEFORE EVERYONE DISAPPEARS FOR GOOD!
WHERE ON EARTH IS THAT CAT WHEN YOU NEED HIM?

TIME TO TRANSFORM.
PLAGG, CLAWS OUT!
TING
FWWSH

LEMME GUESS; WE'RE ALL PLAYING A GAME OF TAG, AND YOU'RE IT?
EXACTLY!
DON'T LET HER TOUCH YOU!
MISSED ME!
JUST A SECOND TOO LATE.
GRR...
HUH?

OOPS...
HEH HEH HEH HEH.
ZWOOSH
NOOO!
SCREECH

AAAH!
FWOOSH
SNAG
KEEP YOUR HANDS TO YOURSELF!
HMPH.
FWISH
OOF!

HA HA HA!
NOW, TIMEBREAKER!
GRAB HER MIRACULOUS! HER EARRING!
YOUR MIRACULOUS IS MINE!
GASP

ZWOOSH
CAT NOIR?!
NOOO!
OH WOW, SIX MINUTES IN ONE GO!
LOOKS LIKE IT'S TIME TO GO BACK AND SAVE MY WATCH!
BLEEP BLEEP

STOP!!!

FWOOSH

WHOOOAA!

AAAAH!

ZWOOSH

WOOHOO!
LAST LAP!

FWOOM
WHOA, WHAT JUST HAPPENED?
GO, ALIX!
YAAY!
OH WOW, WE'VE GONE BACK IN TIME, HAVEN'T WE?
WHATCHA GOT THERE? SOME SUPER OLD CASE OR SOMETHING?
CAREFUL, IT'S ALIX'S!

IF IT'S ALIX'S, IT'S PROBABLY WORTHLESS!
GIVE IT BACK TO ADRIEN, CHLOÉ!
MY WATCH!
CHLOÉ, PUT THE WATCH DOWN!
GASP
EEEEE!

SMASH!
NOOO!
GASP
LADYBUG! THIS TIME, IT'S *YOUR* FAULT!!!
I NEED MORE ENERGY. I GOTTA GO FURTHER BACK IN TIME...

LADYBUG...
...IT'S ALL LADYBUG'S FAULT!

EVERYONE, GET OUT OF HERE!
DON'T LET HER TOUCH YOU!
GRR...
FWWSH
TIME TO TRANSFORM.
WHO ARE YOU?

UH... I DON'T REALLY HAVE TIME TO EXPLAIN RIGHT NOW, BUT I'M YOU FROM JUST A FEW MINUTES IN THE FUTURE!
SHE'S RIGHT!
I CAN FEEL IT! SHE *IS* YOU... FROM THE FUTURE!
CRAZY!
LISTEN, I KNOW IT SEEMS UNBELIEVABLE, BUT TRUST ME.
I MEAN... TRUST... YOURSELF?

OH, AND DAD'S GOING TO CALL ME... ER, YOU, IN TWO MINUTES.
HE WON'T BE HAPPY BECAUSE MRS. CHAMACK IS WAITING FOR YOU OUTSIDE THE BAKERY DOOR.
THE CAKE!
BUT I, I STILL HAVE...
TIME? THAT'S WHAT I THOUGHT, TOO.
MRS. CHAMACK'LL BE EARLY. JUST LEAVE NOW AND TAKE CARE OF THE CAKE, OK?
DON'T
RRY, LADYBUG
N HANDLE THIS
GLE-HANDED!
HOW DO I GET MYSELF INTO THESE CRAZY SITUATIONS?

I CAN'T EXPLAIN NOW, BUT WE'VE GOTTA CAPTURE TIMEBREAKER'S AKUMA. YOUR LIFE DEPENDS ON IT!
WHICH LIFE? I'VE GOT NINE!
I'M SERIOUS! THE AKUMA IS IN H ROLLERBLADES. W GOTTA RELEASE IT!
AM I SEEING DOUBLE ALL OF A SUDDEN?!
ANOTHER THING I DON'T HAVE ENOUGH TIME TO EXPLAIN...

YAAAH!
CLANG
WHA-

I THINK IT'S TIME FOR YOU TO PACK IT IN!
IF WE WERE FASTER, THOSE BOZOS WOULD BE NO MATCH FOR US!
LET'S STOCK UP ON MORE ENERGY FIRST. THEN WE'LL DESTROY THEM!
GASP
ZWICK
ZWOOSH

WOOSH!
WHOOOAAA!!!
FWOOP
HUH?
FWISH
HEY YOU TWO! NEED A HAND?

UH... UH...
THANKS!
BE RIGHT DOWN!
THEY'RE INSANE ON THEIR ROLLERBLADES!
UNSTOPPABLE ON THE GROUND!
SO... WHA THEY'RE **NO** THE GROU
TWO LADYBUGS?!?
I'M IN HEAVEN!

LUCKY CHARM!
ANY IDEAS?!
WHILE YOU TWO FIGURE IT OUT, I'LL TRY TO BUY US SOME TIME!

HMM...
GLACES
DING!
ARE YOU THINKING WHAT I'M THINKING?
OF COURSE!

CATACLYSM!
CRACK!
CRACKLE CRACKLE
BOOM
HUH?!
LET'S FREEZE HER ON OUR WAY PAST!

TIME FOR YOU TO SAY GOODBYE, LADYBUG!
GASP WE'RE STUCK!

HUFF
HUFF
CES

WE'RE GOING TOO FAST!

WE CAN'T STO-

AAAAH!

NOW!

FWOOSH

SNAG
LOOKS LIKE-
-YOUR TIME-
-IS UP!

UGH...
OOF...
SNAP!
SNAP!

CLICK
CLICK
NO MORE EVIL-DOING FOR YOU, LITTLE AKUMA!
TIME TO DE-EVILIZE!
SNAP!
SNAP!
GOTCHA!
CLICK
CLICK

BYE BYE, LITTLE BUTTERFLY!
MIRACULOUS...

...LADYBUG!
FWWSH
FWOOSH
GLACES
FWISH
WHAT THE...?!
FWWSH

POUND IT!
FWOOSH
FWISH
HUH?
HERE. I THINK THIS IS YOURS?
SWEET! HOW DID YOU FIX IT?

THANK YOU! SHOULD NEVER AVE GIVEN IT TO OMEONE ELSE TO LOOK AFTER.
IT WAS MY RESPONSIBILITY. MY BAD.
RESPONSIBILITY 'T SOMETHING TO TAKEN LIGHTLY. I SHOULD KNOW...
YOU'RE TOTALLY RIGHT. I'LL BE MORE CAREFUL NEXT TIME FOR SURE. THANKS, LADYBUG!

I WAS KIND OF GETTING USED TO HAVING TWO LADYBUGS AROUND...
AND NOW YOU'RE GOING TO GET USED TO NO LADYBUGS AROUND.
FWIP
GOTTA SPLIT BEFORE I CHANGE BACK!
-SIGH- SHE'LL FALL FOR ME SOMEDAY. IT'S JUST A MATTER OF TIME...
YOU SLIPPED BY ME THIS TIME, LADYBUG AND CAT NOIR.
BUT ONE DAY, PAST, PRESENT OR FUTURE, YOU *WILL* BE DESTROYED, AND I'LL HAVE YOUR MIRACULOUSES!
I WILL BE UNSTOPPABLE!

HEY! SO, DID YOU HAVE A NICE ANNIVERSARY?
WE SURE DID.
ALTHOUGH, IT *WAS* A CLOSE CALL...?
OH YEAH, MRS. CHAMACK. I'M SORRY THAT I KEPT HER WAITING.
NEXT TIME, PLEASE WAIT FOR THE CUSTOMER IN THE BAKERY AND NOT IN YOUR ROOM, LISTENING TO YOUR LOUD MUSIC!
GOT IT. I PROMISE I WON'T SCREW UP NEXT TIME!
GOOD, BECAUSE MOM'S RIGHT. THERE'S ONLY *ONE* MARINETTE, AND WE'RE COUNTING ON HER!
THE END.